Richard Scarry's BUSYTOWN TREASURY

Random House New York

Compilation copyright © 2016 by the Richard Scarry Corporation
Richard Scarry's Bedtime Stories copyright © 1972, 1978 by Richard Scarry
Richard Scarry's Please and Thank You Book copyright © 1973 by Richard Scarry
Richard Scarry's A Day at the Fire Station copyright © 2003 by the Richard Scarry Corporation
Richard Scarry's A Day at the Police Station copyright © 2004 by the Richard Scarry Corporation
Richard Scarry's A Day at the Airport copyright © 2001 by the Richard Scarry Corporation
Nicky Goes to the Doctor copyright © 1972, 1978 by Richard Scarry

All rights reserved. Published in the United States by Random House Children's Books, a division
of Penguin Random House LLC, 1745 Broadway, New York, NY 10019, and in Canada by
Penguin Random House Canada Limited, Toronto.

Random House and the colophon are registered trademarks of Penguin Random House LLC.

Visit us on the Web!
randomhousekids.com
RichardScarryBooks.com

Educators and librarians, for a variety of teaching tools, visit us at RHTeachersLibrarians.com

Library of Congress Control Number: 2016933092
ISBN 978-0-553-53899-1

MANUFACTURED IN CHINA
10 9 8 7 6 5 4 3 2 1

Contents

Richard Scarry's
BEDTiME STORiES

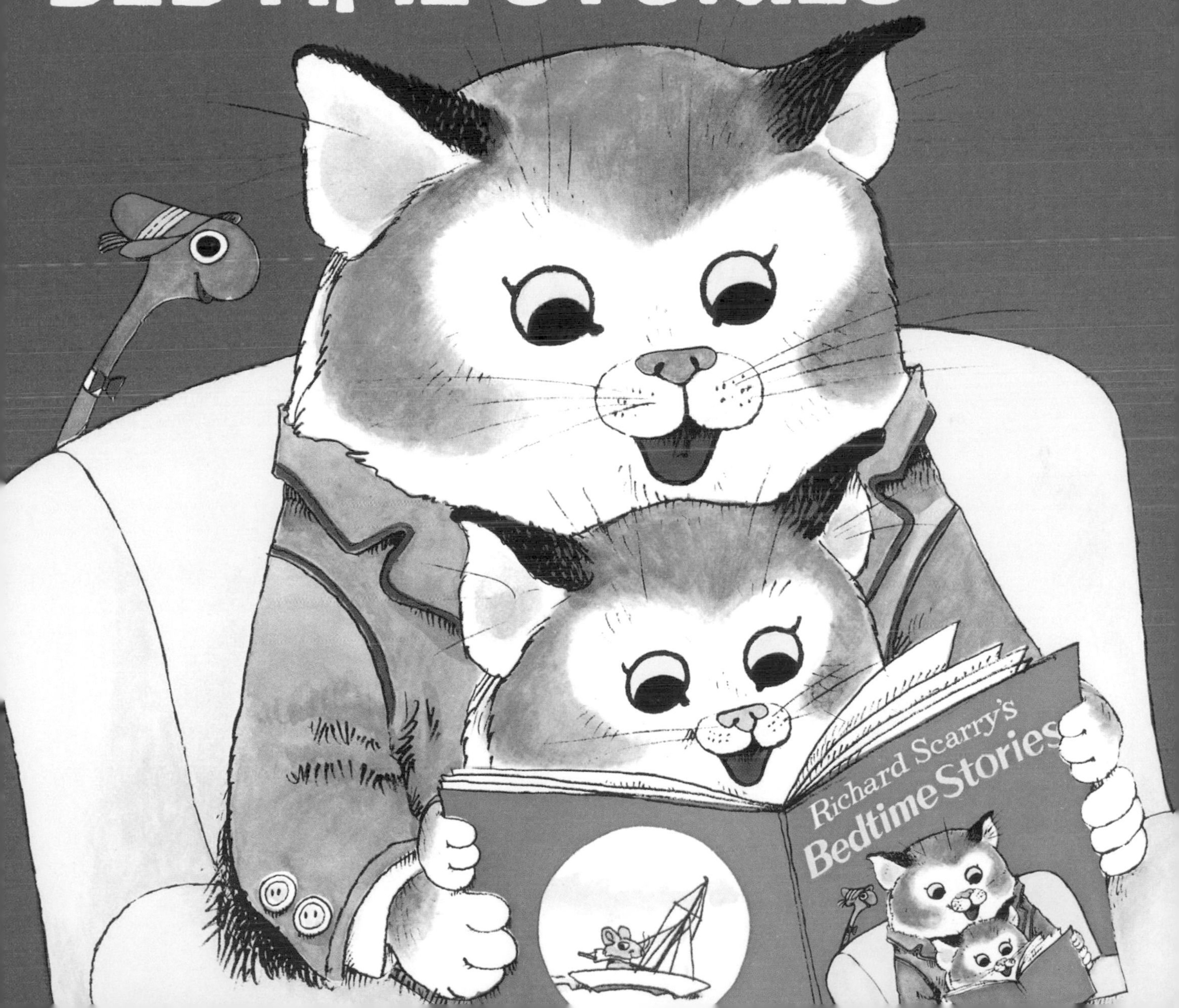

Uncle Willy and the Pirates

Not a soul dared to go sailing. Do you know why?

There was a wicked band of pirates about, and they would steal anything they could get their hands on!

But Uncle Willy wasn't afraid. "They won't bother me," he said.

He dropped his anchor near a deserted island. Aunty Pastry had baked him a pie for his lunch.

"I think I will have a little nap before I eat my pie," said Uncle Willy to himself.

Uncle Willy went to sleep. *B-z-z-z-z*. What is THAT I see
climbing on board? A PIRATE! And another! And another?
PIRATES, UNCLE WILLY!
Uncle Willy couldn't do a thing. There were just too many pirates.

First, they put Uncle Willy on the deserted island. Then they started to eat his pie.

"M-m-m! DEE-licious!" they all said.

Uncle Willy was furious. He didn't care so much about the pie. But he needed his boat to get home again.

Then he had an idea. He gathered some branches, some sea shells, and some long beach grass. He wove the beach grass into a kind of cloth.

He tied some sea shells
onto the branches and made
a ferocious-looking mouth.

He tied the grass cloth onto the mouth,
then attached some sea-shell eyes.
By the time he tied on a spiky palm leaf,
he had made a ferocious MONSTER!

Uncle Willy got inside.
He was now "Uncle Willy,
THE FEROCIOUS MONSTER."
Look out, you pirates!

11

The Ferocious Monster swam out to the boat. The pirates were terrified. They all ran into the cabin.

The Ferocious Monster closed the door behind them—and locked it. The Monster had captured the wicked pirates! Then he sailed back home.

Aunty Pastry was on the dock.
"There is a horrible monster coming!"
she cried. "He is even worse than the pirates!"

Uncle Willy took off his monster suit. Everyone said,
"Thank goodness it was only you!"
Sergeant Murphy took the pirates away to be punished.
Well . . . Uncle Willy had made the seas safe to sail on again.
Hurray for Uncle Willy—THE FEROCIOUS MONSTER!

How was the pie, Uncle Willy?

You BAD. pie rats!!!

Sergeant Murphy
and the Banana Thief

Sergeant Murphy was busy putting parking tickets on cars when, suddenly, who should come running out of the market but Bananas Gorilla. He had stolen a bunch of bananas and was trying to escape.

Murphy! LOOK! He is stealing your motorcycle, too!

B-r-e-e-e-t!

Sergeant Murphy was furious.
Huckle and Lowly Worm had been watching.
Huckle said, "You may borrow my tricycle
to chase after him if you want to."

Away they went . . . chasing after
that naughty thief.

15

They raced through the crowded streets.
Don't YOU ever ride your tricycle in the street!

They crossed a drawbridge just as it
was opening to let a boat go through.

Bananas stopped suddenly and went into a restaurant.

Murphy said to Louie, the owner, "I am looking for a thief!"
Together, they searched the whole restaurant. But they couldn't
find Bananas anywhere.

Louie then said, "Sit down and relax, Murphy. I will bring
you and your friends something delicious to eat."

Somebody had better pick up those banana peels
before someone slips on one. Don't you think so?

Louie brought them a bowl of banana soup. Lowly said, "I'll bet Bananas Gorilla would like to be here right now."

"Huckle, we mustn't forget to wash our hands before eating," said Sergeant Murphy. So they walked back to the washroom. Lowly went along, too.

When they came back, they discovered that their table had disappeared.

Indeed, it was slowly creeping away . . . when it slipped on a banana peel!
And guess who was hiding underneath.

Sergeant Murphy, we are
very proud of you!
Bananas must be punished.
Someday he has to learn that
it is naughty to steal things.

Ma Pig's New Car

Pa Pig bought a new car for Ma Pig. She will certainly be surprised when she sees her new car, won't she?

On the way home, Pa stopped at a drugstore.

When he came out, he got into a jeep by mistake.
(You should be wearing your glasses, Pa Pig!)
Harry and Sally thought that Pa had swapped cars with a soldier.

Stop, thief!

Then Pa went to the market. When he came out, he got into a police car.
"You made a good swap, Daddy," said Harry. But Pa wasn't listening . . .
and he didn't seem to be thinking very well either. Don't you agree?

Next Pa drove to a fruit stand to buy some apples. When he left
he took Farmer Fox's tractor. My, but Pa is absentminded, isn't he?
"Ma will certainly like her new tractor," said Sally to Harry.

They stopped to watch a fire.
When the fire was out they left—
in the fire engine! How can *anyone*
make so many mistakes?

Hey, Joe! You forgot to turn off the motor.

Then they stopped to watch some workers
who were digging a big hole in the ground.
No! Pa did NOT get into that dump truck.
But by mistake, he got into . . .

. . . Roger Rhino's power shovel!
Ma Pig was certainly surprised to see her new CAR!
But Pa! Do you know how to stop it?

Yes, he did!

Oh, oh! Here comes Roger now.
He has found Ma Pig's new car
and is bringing it to her. It looks
as though he is very angry with that
someone who took his power shovel.

ROGER! PLEASE BE CAREFUL! You are squeezing Ma's little car just a little bit too tightly.

Well, let's all hope that Pa Pig will never again make *that* many mistakes in one day!

The Three Fishermen

Lowly, Huckle, and Daddy were going fishing.

Their little motorboat took them
far away from shore.

Daddy said, "Throw out the anchor, Lowly."
Lowly threw the anchor out . . . and himself with it!

27

Lowly climbed back in and Daddy began to fish.

Daddy caught an old bicycle.
But he didn't want an old bicycle.
He wanted a fish.

Suddenly Huckle fell overboard.
Wouldn't you know that something
like that would happen?

Daddy pulled Huckle out. Why, look there!
Huckle caught a fish in his pants!

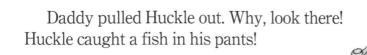

Daddy fished some more.
But he couldn't catch anything.
He was disgusted.
"Let's go home," he said.
"There just aren't any fish
down there."

As Daddy was getting out of the boat,
he slipped . . . and fell!
Oh, boy! Is he ever mad now!

But why is he yelling so loudly?

Aha! I see! A fish was biting his tail. The fish was trying to catch Daddy. It is good that Daddy has a strong tail. Now Lowly is the only one who hasn't caught . . .

But look!
Lowly has taken off
his hat. Do you see
what is under it?
A FISH!
Very good, Lowly.

Yes, there you see three
very good fishermen!

The Unlucky Day

Mr. Raccoon opened his eyes. "Wake up, Mamma," he said.
"It looks like a good day."

He turned on the water. The faucet broke off.

"I'd better call Mr. Fixit," he said.

He sat down to breakfast. He burned his toast. Mamma
burned the bacon.

Mamma asked him to bring home food for supper. As he
was leaving, the door fell off its hinges.

Driving down the road, Mr. Raccoon had a flat tire.
While he was fixing it, his pants ripped.

He started again. His car motor exploded and wouldn't go any farther.
He decided to walk. The wind blew his hat away. Bye-bye, hat!

"I must try to be more careful," thought Mr. Raccoon.
"This is turning into a bad day."

His friend Warty Wart Hog came up behind him and patted him on the back. Warty! Don't pat so hard!
"Let's go to a restaurant for lunch," said Warty.

Warty ate and ate and ate. Have you ever seen such bad manners? Take off your hat, Warty!

Warty left without paying for his food. Mr. Raccoon had to pay for it. Just look at all the plates that Warty used!

Mr. Raccoon wondered, "What other bad things can happen to me today?"

Well . . . for one thing, the tablecloth could catch on his belt buckle!

"Don't you ever come in here again!" the waiter shouted.

"I think I had better get home as quickly as possible," thought Mr. Raccoon.

"I don't want to get into any *more* trouble."

He arrived home just as Mr. Fixit was leaving.
Mr. Fixit had spent the entire day finding new leaks.
"I will come back tomorrow to fix the leaks," said Mr. Fixit.

Mrs. Raccoon asked her husband if he had brought home
the food she had asked for. She wanted to cook something hot
for supper. Of course Mr. Raccoon hadn't, so they had to eat
cold pickles for supper.

After supper they went upstairs to bed.
"There isn't another unlucky thing that
can happen to me today," said Mr. Raccoon
as he got into bed. Oh, dear! His bed broke!

I do hope that Mr. Raccoon will have a
better day tomorrow, don't you?

Richard Scarry's Please and Thank You Book

THE BUSY DAY

Huckle and Lowly got out of bed.
They washed their faces and brushed their teeth.

(Lowly didn't have any hair to comb.)

After dressing, they put
away their pajamas very neatly.

At breakfast, they chewed
their food slowly and quietly.

When they had finished,
they asked to be excused
from the table. *Everyone*
helped Mommy to clear the table.

Thank you, Lowly.

Then all the children went off to school.
Little Sister's shoelace came untied.
Everybody waited while Lowly tied it for her.

At school their teacher
was waiting to greet them.
"Good morning, Miss Honey,"
they all said, cheerfully.

Miss Honey asked them to copy
some words from the blackboard.
When they were done, Lowly
helped Miss Honey by cleaning off
the blackboard.

cat

39

During recess they all went out
into the schoolyard to play.
They took turns going down the slide.

(That Lowly is certainly a fine slider, isn't he?)

In the afternoon everyone cut up
pieces of colored paper and pasted
them together to make pictures.

B-R-I-I-N-N-G-G! The school bell rang.
Time to go home! Lowly helped Little Sister
clean up her desk. He takes good care of her
because she is younger than the others.
Don't spill the paste, Lowly!

On the way home, Lowly
fell into a mud puddle.
Poor Lowly!

40

He left muddy footprints
all over Mother Cat's clean floor.
"Lowly," said Mother Cat.
"You *know* you should never come
into the house with a muddy foot."

She had to give Lowly a bath.
My! He's a slippery little fellow.

Brrrrr!

Then she dried him off,
and he got dressed for supper.

At the supper table, everyone
ate with his fork. Nobody ever
eats with his fingers or his foot.

After supper Daddy gave everyone
a piggyback ride to bed.
Good night, all!

41

PIG WILL
AND
PIG WON'T

Mother Pig had two little pigs—
Pig Will and Pig Won't.
Whenever she asked them to do something, Pig Will said, "I will."
But Pig Won't always said, "I WON'T!"

If Daddy asked them to play more quietly,
Pig Will said, "I will." But Pig Won't always said, "I WON'T!"

When Mother asked, "Will someone please empty
the wastebasket?" who do you suppose said, "I will"?

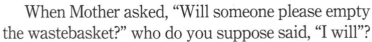

One day Daddy said, "Who will come to the boatyard
and help me work on my boat?"
Pig Will said, "I will."
Guess who said, "I won't."

So Daddy and Pig Will drove
to the boatyard to work.
And Pig Won't stayed home.

Mother Pig stayed in her room
all afternoon writing a children's book.
She paid no attention to Pig Won't.

He had no one to play with.
He had no one to talk to.
Pig Won't spent a very boring
afternoon.

But everyone at the boatyard
was working together busily
and having a good time.

Pig Will helped
Daddy paint his boat.

He helped Bananas Gorilla
build a Bananaboat.

He helped Sally Bunny
varnish her water skis.

Willy Bear hoisted him
to the top of the mast
on his sailboat. There
Pig Will fixed
the wind vane.

Hard workers get very hungry.
So everyone stopped to have ice cream.
(Oh, dear! Somebody forgot to bring the napkins.)

45

When Pig Will got back home, he told Pig Won't about the good time he had had. Suddenly Pig Won't began to understand that work—especially if you are helping others—can be lots more fun than doing nothing.

"I must stop saying 'I won't' all the time," he told himself.

Well . . . the very next day his mother asked if someone would help her sweep.

Right away Pig Will said, "I will."

And right away Pig Won't said, "ME TOO!"

I will!

ME TOO!

So from that day on, Pig Won't has always been called "Pig Me Too"!

46

A VISIT WITH TILLIE

Tillie called some friends and invited them to her house for a little tea party. Bugdozer was already there.

When they arrived at Tillie's house, Huckle shook hands with her and said politely, "How do you do?" The other guests all did the same.

All, that is, except Lowly.
He had to shake his foot with Tillie.

Harry Hyena picked up Tillie's big, beautiful vase and waved it around. Tillie had to ask him to put it down. It isn't a good idea to pick up other people's valuable things without asking permission.

Then Tillie asked them all to sit down while she went to get some cake and ice cream.

"Lowly! Stop rocking back and forth in that chair!" said Little Sister. "You are supposed to sit up straight when you are eating at the table."

When Tillie brought in the cake, she asked Lowly to get her a chair.

48

Lowly brought her a chair.
But it was his own tiny chair
instead of Tillie's BIG chair!

CRASH! Just look what happened.
"Oh, my," said Lowly. "That's
one chair I'll never rock on again."
Tillie laughed. "You won't be
able to *sit* on it again either,"
she said.
Then they all laughed.
They were glad Tillie wasn't angry.

When the party was over,
they all said, "Thank you
for the very nice time, Tillie."
And Lowly even blew her a kiss.

SERGEANT MURPHY'S SAFETY RULES

Here is an old friend—Sergeant Murphy. He has a few good rules everybody should learn . . . and obey.

Always fasten your seat belt in case the car stops suddenly. Little Sister's doll wasn't wearing a seat belt. Poor dolly!

Cross the street at the crosswalk when the light tells you that you should.

Never chase a ball into the road.
You might be hit by a car.
Ask an older person
to get the ball for you.

Don't lean out of the window
when you are riding in a car.

Don't run on crowded sidewalks.
Don't push people either—even
for fun. Someone may get hurt.

51

Don't play near the water.
Sergeant Murphy had to jump
into the water to save Ralphie
Raccoon. Very good, Murphy!

Don't throw sticks or stones at people.
You can hurt somebody that way.

Sergeant Murphy had to put
a bandage on Walter's head.
He bought him an ice cream cone,
too. Wasn't that nice?

Never, never play with matches.
Sergeant Murphy arrived just in time
with that hose!

Sergeant Murphy tells his family to be
careful at home, too. His little girl, Bridget,
knows she should stay away from the hot
stove when Mrs. Murphy is cooking.

But Bridget doesn't know she should
not leave toys lying on the stairs.
Poor Sergeant Murphy!

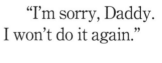

"I'm sorry, Daddy.
I won't do it again."

DOLLY'S BIRTHDAY PARTY

Lowly, Huckle, and Little Sister were all invited to Dolly Pig's birthday party.

They brought birthday presents to give to Dolly, and they put on their very best clothes.

When they arrived at Dolly's house, they all said, "Happy Birthday, Dolly." And Lowly said, "That is a very pretty dress, Dolly."

When Dolly began to open her gifts, her brother cried because he didn't have any presents. He should be patient. When his birthday comes, he will have lots of presents to open, too.
Dolly thanked everybody for the gifts.

Then came the birthday cake.
First, Dolly made a wish.
After that she blew out the candles.
(She almost blew away the cake!)

They could hardly wait to eat the beautiful birthday cake. And the ice cream, too! Lowly loves ice cream. Do you?

Later, they played Pin the Tail on the Donkey. Each child took a turn, and the youngest went first. That is the polite way to do things.

Who do you suppose won? . . . LOWLY! He pinned the tail closest to where it was supposed to go. He won a very nice prize, too.

But *somebody* must have thought Lowly was the donkey. Look at his tail! "Ha! Ha! Ha!" laughed Lowly. "What a crazy donkey *I* am!"

At last it was time for the party to end. Lowly remembered to say to Dolly and her mother, "Thank you for a very nice time." He is a very polite little donkey, isn't he?

57

LOWLY WORM'S HORRID PESTS

Lowly Worm knows some really Horrid Pests.
He hopes you aren't one of them.

Be careful! You'll break it!

Here is a Selfish Pest.
He won't share his tricycle with his friend.

Who threw that?

This is a Litterbug Pest.
He throws his rubbish everywhere.

PLEASE PLACE RUBBISH HERE

horrors!

And here is a Gobbling Pest.
Don't be like that rude fellow.
Take small bites and chew slowly.
Keep your mouth closed while eating.

I would never eat like _that_!

You
cad!

Look at the Grabby Pest!
He took Little Sister's ice cream, but
Grandma is going to catch him with her
umbrella. Don't take things that don't
belong to you.

Never pick on children
smaller than you are.
That is being a mean Bully Pest.

You leave
my brother
alone!

59

Don't start to talk
when others are already
talking. You will be an
Interrupting Pest.

Just say politely,
"May I ask you something?"
Or, "May I tell you something
about that?"

Stop teasing Lowly!
He's my friend!

A Teasing Pest is just awful!
Nobody likes to be called names.
And sticking out your tongue isn't
very pretty either.

A Noisy Pest is always shouting
and giving people headaches.
No one likes to have a headache.

Lowly also hates Quarreling Pests . . .

and Fighting Pests . . .

and Smashing Pests!
They spoil all the fun.

And don't be a Cry Baby Pest
when you lose at games or don't
get what you want.
Lowly Worm *never* cries!

Be a
good
loser!

There are also Driving People Crazy Pests. When their parents tell them they can't do something, these pests just keep pestering and saying, "Why? . . . Why can't I?" over and over again.

Whining Pests are very annoying, too. Don't whine and carry on if something doesn't work the first time you try it.

Let's go!

Well, that's enough pests. Let's look at some Good Friends and Neighbors for a change.

GOOD FRIENDS and NEIGHBORS

Good Friends and Neighbors always help each other.
Right now all the Bunny Family are trying to help Grandma
find her glasses. Where in the world could she have put them?

Pig Will and Pig Me Too are
also Good Neighbors. When someone
asks them to do something, they
do it right away—with a big smile.

AAAACHOOO!

Good Friends always cover their noses when sneezing or coughing. But it's hard for Eddie Elephant to cover *his* nose when he sneezes. Look out for germs, everyone!

What does Lowly always say when he asks for something?

Please?
May I?

And what does Lowly say when someone gives him something?
Do you say that, too? Good for you!

Thank you!

If you have a friend who is sick, visit him or send him a card. Tell him you hope he gets well soon.

Share with others if you would like others to share with you.

Everyone likes to receive presents. Give a present to someone once in a while. Kisses make very nice presents. But don't be stingy. Give a BIG kiss!

When you are leaving somebody's house after a visit, always remember to say, "Thank you for the very nice time."

Lowly even blows a kiss when *he* leaves.

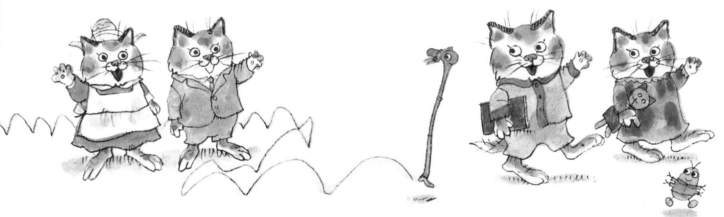

Go to bed as soon as your parents tell you it is time. No one should have to be told a dozen times.

All right, Lowly!
Please take off your hat
and shoe when you go to bed.
Good night, everyone.
Sleep tight!

Just a minute!
I have to get a glass of water!

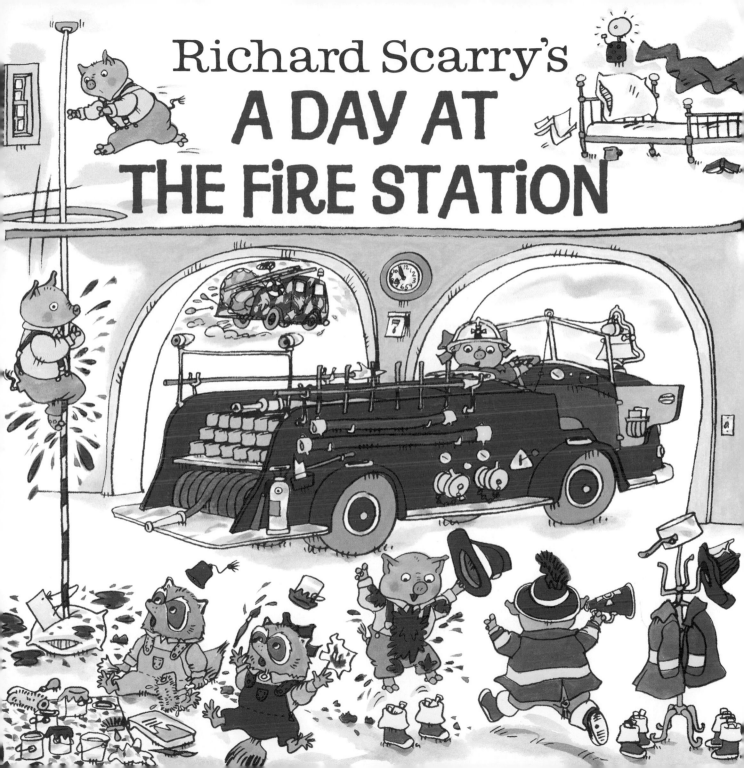

Richard Scarry's
A DAY AT THE FIRE STATION

"Wonderful!" replies Chief Smokey.

Drippy and Sticky, the housepainters,
pull up in front of the Busytown fire station.
"We're here to paint the firehouse!"
says Drippy.

"But please don't park your paint truck in front of the firehouse doors," Smokey says. "We firefighters have to be able to drive out at ANY time."

After parking their paint truck
out of the way, Drippy and Sticky
enter the fire station.

"Wow! What a nifty place!" says Drippy.

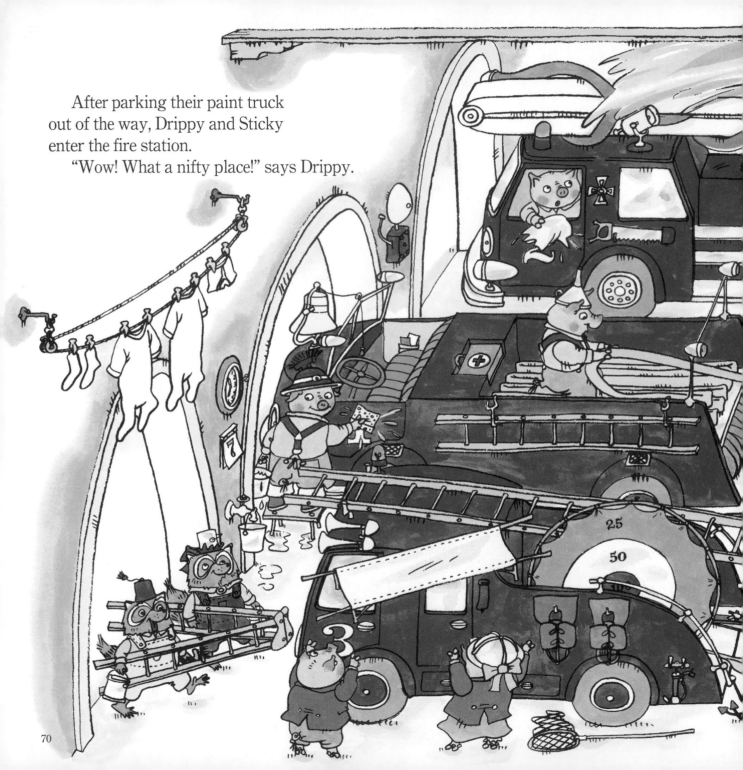

The firefighters are busy cleaning their fire engines.
"We firefighters like to keep our engines nice and clean,
so please be careful not to get any paint on them,"
says Smokey.

"Aye-aye, sir!" replies Sticky.

Drippy covers a fire engine with a big cloth so that it won't get dripped on. Sticky opens the cans of paint.

Drippy begins to paint the firehouse ceiling pink.
Sticky starts to paint the firehouse poles in candy stripes.

Oops! Drippy's cloth seems to have slipped off the fire engine.

"My red fire engine!" shouts Smokey. "It's pink!"

"Don't worry," says Drippy. "We'll have your fire engine cleaned up in no time."

But instead of rubbing off, the wet paint smears in long streaks. What a mess!

RRRINNG! RRRINNG! sounds a loud bell. It's the fire station alarm!

The firefighters sleeping in the dormitory upstairs leap from their beds and slide down the poles to the engines below.

"Oh, no!" shout Drippy and Sticky.
"Oh, no!" shout the firefighters,
covered in candy-stripe paint.

74

But stained uniforms or no, the brave firefighters jump into their boots, grab their coats and helmets, and charge out of the fire station aboard their red—and pink—fire engines. WWWRRRR! CLANG! CLANG!

"Well," says Drippy, "now that the firefighters are gone, perhaps we can get our painting done."

The firefighters have been called out to a traffic accident. Cecelia's cement mixer bumped into Horace's honey truck and knocked over Farmer Hal's haywagon. What a gooey mess!

Thank goodness for the firefighters! They will have everything cleaned up in no time.

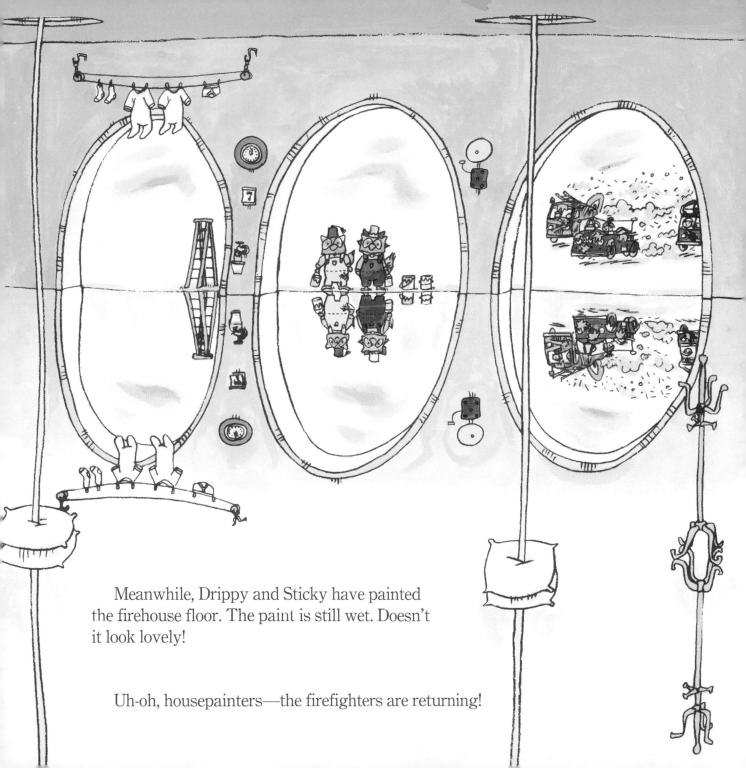

Meanwhile, Drippy and Sticky have painted the firehouse floor. The paint is still wet. Doesn't it look lovely!

Uh-oh, housepainters—the firefighters are returning!

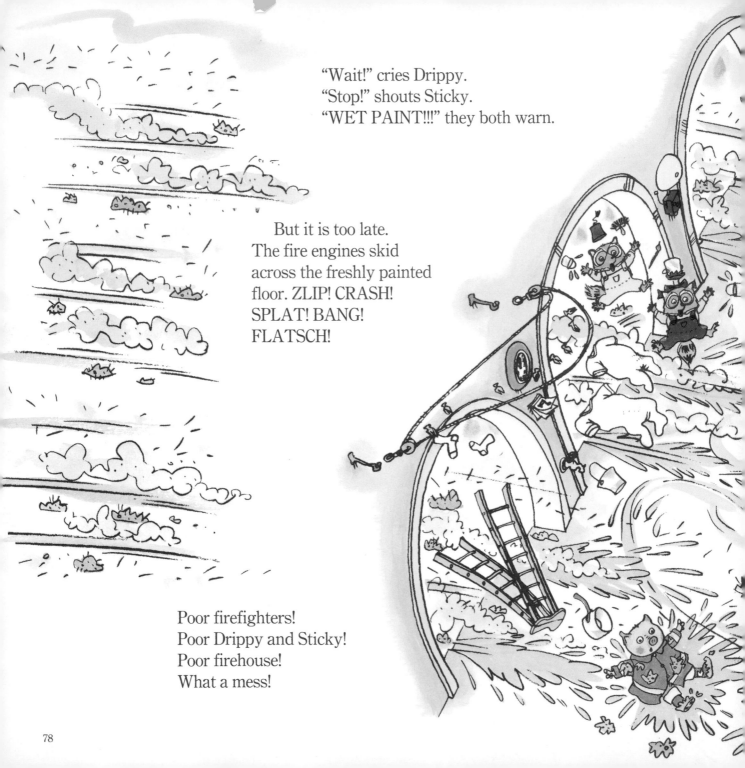

"Wait!" cries Drippy.
"Stop!" shouts Sticky.
"WET PAINT!!!" they both warn.

But it is too late.
The fire engines skid
across the freshly painted
floor. ZLIP! CRASH!
SPLAT! BANG!
FLATSCH!

Poor firefighters!
Poor Drippy and Sticky!
Poor firehouse!
What a mess!

Straw and cement and honey are EVERYWHERE.

Smokey picks up a hose and sprays out the fire station. SWWIIIIIIIISH! SWWOOOOOSH!

Suddenly, there is another alarm.
This time, it's a fire!

The firefighters throw all their equipment
into the fire engines and are off to the rescue.

82

Look! It's a fire at Vesuvio's Peppery Pizza Parlor! The firefighters quickly hook up the pumper engine to the fire hydrant and bravely rush inside.

83

The fire is in the oven! (It's a burnt pizza.)
Hurry, firefighters!
With a spray of water from the hose, the fire is put out.

To thank the firefighters, Vesuvio invites
them all to a big pizza lunch. Isn't he nice?

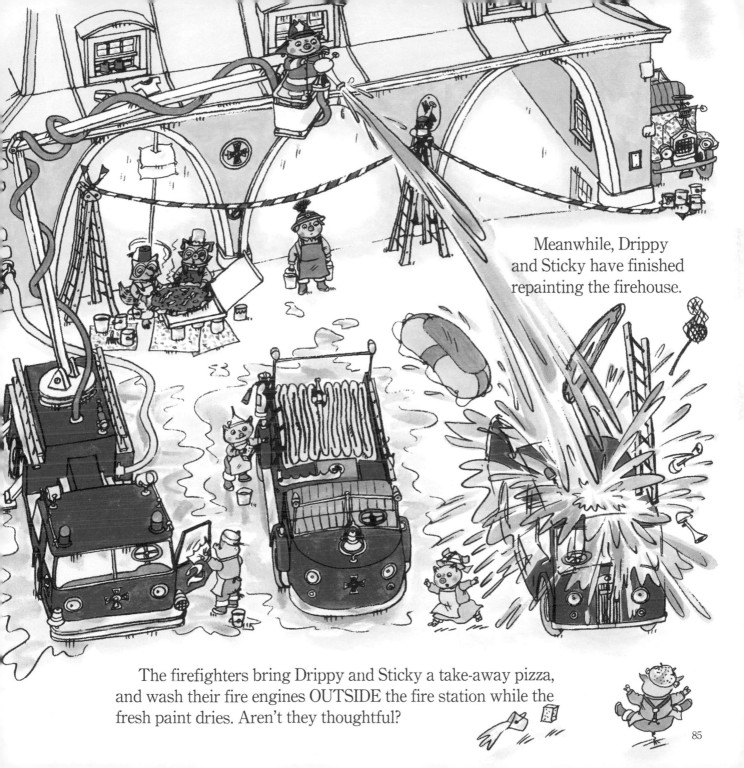

Meanwhile, Drippy and Sticky have finished repainting the firehouse.

The firefighters bring Drippy and Sticky a take-away pizza, and wash their fire engines OUTSIDE the fire station while the fresh paint dries. Aren't they thoughtful?

85

STICK
THE BERRY · WITH
BEST!

TAM'S

Just then, Tammy Tapir drives up
in her strawberry jam truck.
"Can anyone please tell me how
to get to the thruway from here?"
Tammy asks the firefighters.

Uh-oh. Isn't that Roger Rhino's
wrecking crane coming?
Hey, slow down there, Roger!

JAMS

TAM'S · JAMS

Jammy

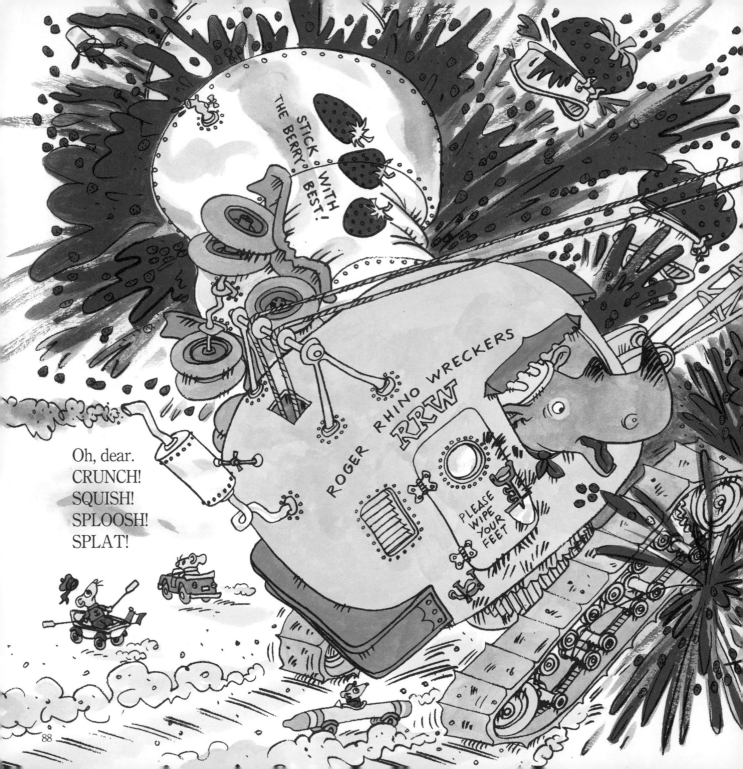

Oh, dear.
CRUNCH!
SQUISH!
SPLOOSH!
SPLAT!

88

Nice work, Roger!

"Gee, I'm awfully sorry about this," says Roger, apologizing.
"Oh, don't worry," says Smokey with a sigh. "We'll have
this cleaned up in no time. It's all in a firefighter's day
at the fire station."

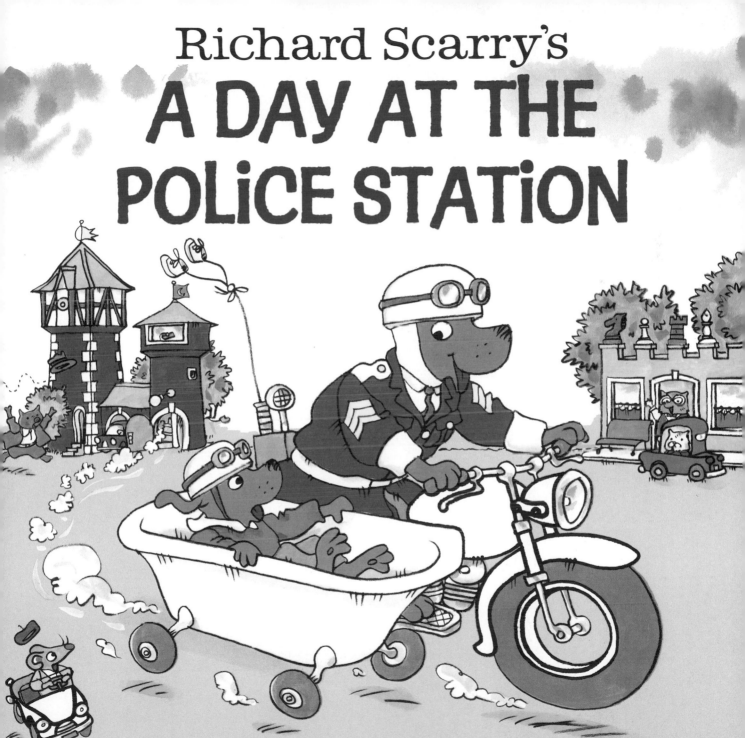

It is Friday evening.
The Murphy family has finished
dinner. Mrs. Murphy clears the table while
Sergeant Murphy washes the dishes.

"It's time to get into your
pajamas and go off to bed,"
Mrs. Murphy tells Bridget.

"Run along up to your room, and I'll read
you a story!" calls Sergeant Murphy.

While Bridget climbs the stairs, she can hear her parents talking in the kitchen.

"I have to go to Workville tomorrow, Sarge," says Mrs. Murphy. "Could you please look after Bridget?"

"Hmmm," replies Sergeant Murphy. "Officer Flo is sick. I have to be on duty for her tomorrow—but I'll just take Bridget to the police station with me. She won't mind, I think."

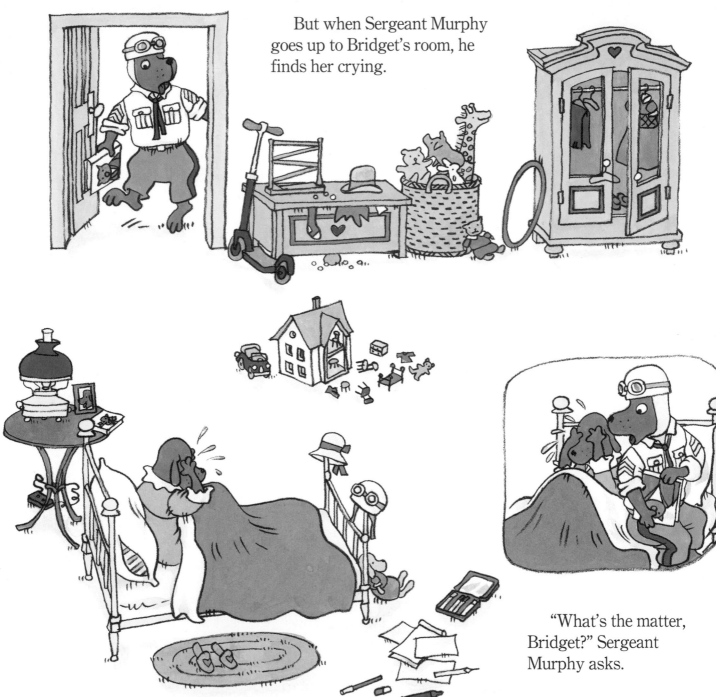

But when Sergeant Murphy goes up to Bridget's room, he finds her crying.

"What's the matter, Bridget?" Sergeant Murphy asks.

"I wanted to go to the amusement park tomorrow," Bridget cries. "And now you have to work! I don't like that you're a police officer. You're ALWAYS on duty!"

"But being a police officer is very important," says Sergeant Murphy, hugging Bridget. "I'm sorry we can't go to the amusement park, but we'll have a good time at the police station. THAT I can promise!"

The next morning,
Sergeant Murphy and Bridget
drive off to the police station.
"Goodbye, Bridget!" calls
Mrs. Murphy. "Goodbye, Sarge!"

On the way, they
come to an intersection.
There is a huge traffic jam!
The traffic light
is broken.

Sergeant Murphy
directs the cars
until Mr. Fixit
can come and
repair the light.

"This is what Daddy calls
a good time?" Bridget says, pouting.
"Watching traffic?"

Just then, Mr. Raccoon
comes out of his coffee shop,
bringing Bridget a glass
of milk and a donut.

"Your father sure does a great job, Bridget!" he says.
"I don't know what Busytown would do without him."

Soon Sergeant Murphy and Bridget are on their way again. When they arrive at the police station, the telephone is ringing.

Sergeant Murphy answers it. "Busytown police station. Sergeant Murphy here."

99

It's Hilda Hippo on the line.

"Oh, Sergeant Murphy, I'm so frightened!
There's a ghost in my bathroom!"
"A GHOST?" Sergeant Murphy replies.
"Just stay calm, Hilda. I'll be right over!"

Sergeant Murphy
and Bridget race over to Hilda's.

When they arrive, Hilda looks as pale as a ghost herself.

"Sergeant Murphy, I haven't slept a wink!" Hilda says nervously. "The ghost has been flushing the toilet all night!"

Suddenly, from upstairs comes:

FLUSH!

"Hmmm," says Sergeant Murphy. "You two wait here while I see about this—er—ghost."

He peeks inside,
but the bathroom
is empty.

FLUSH!

goes the toilet again.
Sergeant Murphy
climbs onto the toilet
seat and checks inside
the tank.

"There!" he says.

"The toilet just needed some
adjusting. You shouldn't let your
imagination run away with you
like that, Hilda!"

On the way back to the police station, they
see a toddler crying in the street.

Sergeant Murphy takes her to the police station.

The phone is ringing when they
arrive. It's the child's mother!
Thank goodness her darling is safe
with Sergeant Murphy. Bridget
plays with the toddler until
her mother comes to fetch her.

Just then, Mr. Frumble arrives at the door. "Excuse me, but has anyone seen my hat?" he asks. "It's the third one I've lost in three days!"

Sergeant Murphy makes a note of the lost hat and promises to call Mr. Frumble if it's found.

Minutes after Mr. Frumble leaves, Mr. Gronkle storms in.

"I'm here to report a robbery!" he shouts.

"Wow! A real robbery!" thinks Bridget.

"My car keys have been stolen," says Mr. Gronkle, "and I know who took them: Wolfgang Wolf, Harry Hyena, and Benny Baboon!"

Through the door come Wolfgang, Harry, and Benny—each wearing a green hat.

"Did somebody call us?" asks Wolfgang.

"We found these hats," says Harry. "And we're bringing them here to be returned to their rightful owner!" adds Benny.

"I saw you thieves walking around my car," shouts Mr. Gronkle. "You must have stolen my keys! I can't find them anywhere!"

"Now, just a moment, Mr. Gronkle!"
Sergeant Murphy says. "You have to
have some proof before you can accuse
someone of stealing."

"We didn't take your keys!"
says Wolfgang.
"We'd never steal anything!"
says Harry.
"Honest!" adds Benny.

Sergeant Murphy decides they should all go
together to the scene of the crime.

"Are THESE your stolen keys?"
Bridget asks Mr. Gronkle,
holding up a ring of keys.

"Why, yes!" replies
Mr. Gronkle, surprised.
"Wherever did you
find them?"

"Under your car, by the door," says Bridget.

"I guess your 'thief' must have accidentally
dropped them," Sergeant Murphy tells
Mr. Gronkle.

"I owe you an apology," Mr. Gronkle
says to Wolfgang, Harry, and Benny.
"To make up for my mistake, I want to
take you out for sundaes."

As they walk back to the police station, Sergeant Murphy and Bridget see two boys fighting.

Sergeant Murphy runs up and pulls them apart. "Stop that!" he says. "What's this all about?"

"Jimmy won't let me ride his bike!" says Johnny.
"It's MY bike!" shouts Jimmy.

"You need to settle your problems peacefully," Sergeant Murphy tells the boys.

Just then, Bridget hears someone crying, "HELP!"

Sergeant Murphy races
to the edge of the pier.
He bravely dives into
the river!

Sergeant Murphy carries
Bananas Gorilla safely out of
the river.
My, isn't he strong!

Then he dives back into the river!
Does he want to go for a swim?

No! He wants to get
Bananas's Bananamobile!
"Please do be careful
when driving near the water,"
Sergeant Murphy tells Bananas.

Back at the police
station, Sergeant Murphy
puts on a dry uniform.
"We have to hurry, or we'll
be late for school!" he says.

Bridget is confused.
"School? On Saturday?" she wonders.

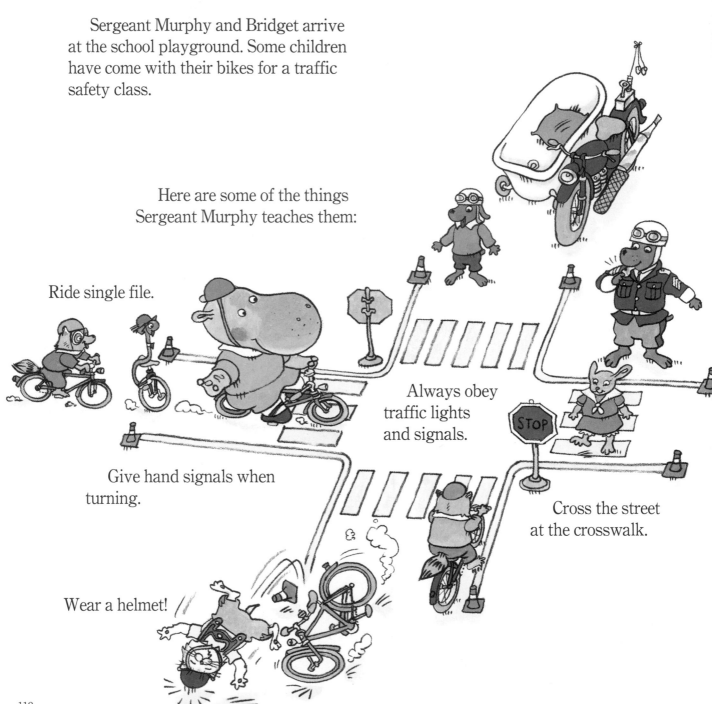

Sergeant Murphy and Bridget arrive at the school playground. Some children have come with their bikes for a traffic safety class.

Here are some of the things Sergeant Murphy teaches them:

Ride single file.

Always obey traffic lights and signals.

Give hand signals when turning.

Cross the street at the crosswalk.

Wear a helmet!

STOP

Make sure your brakes, lights, and bell work properly.

And please don't leave
your bike lying around.

Park it properly. Thank you!

"We missed you at the amusement park today, Bridget," Huckle says.
"I was on duty with Daddy all day!" Bridget replies. "We got rid of a
ghost and helped a little girl find her mommy. Then we solved a robbery,
and Daddy stopped two boys who were fighting. Then he bravely saved
Bananas Gorilla from drowning!"

"Wow!" says Huckle. "Having a dad who's a police officer must be pretty neat!"

"You bet it is!" replies Bridget. "I think my daddy has the very best job EVER!"

"Um—excuse me, Sergeant Murphy, but has anyone seen my hat yet?"

Father Cat wants to take Huckle,
Sally, and Lowly out sailing this afternoon.
Plink! Plop! Plink!
Uh-oh, Father Cat, it's starting to rain.

"I guess that's the end of our sailing
today!" says Father Cat.

He puts the
top up on the car.

"There's nothing to do but go back home."

What a
disappointment.

Father Cat stops at Scotty's Filling Station for gasoline.
"Fill 'er up, please, Scotty!" Father Cat says.
Just then, Rudolf Von Flugel drives up in his airplane-car.
"Good afternoon, Father Cat!" says Rudolf. "Are you going sailing?"

"No, we're going home, Rudolf," Father Cat says sadly. "The children will have to play inside today."

"Hmm," says Rudolf. "Why don't they come with me? I'm going to the airport. There's lots to see there, even when it rains!"

"Wow! Can we, Dad?" Huckle asks.

Father Cat thinks it is a great idea. He helps place the children in Rudolf's airplane-car.

"Don't worry, Father Cat. I'll bring the children home dry as baked apple strudel!" says Rudolf.

And off they go! *Brruumm!*

119

runway

radar

pier

catering
truck

control
tower

snowplow

catering
kitchen

airport bus

They arrive at the airport in no time.

120

wind sock

runway lights

hangar

a tractor towing a plane

restaurant

departure terminal

parking garage

ARRIVALS DEPARTURES

arrivals

taxis

My, what a busy place it is!

121

check-in counters

conveyor belt

TO PARIS ⬇

TO NEW YORK ⬇

TO VENICE ⬇

scale

luggage cart

"Here we are!" Rudolf says, driving into the departure terminal.

CLOSED ✕

TO WORKVILLE ⬇

TO THE GATES ➡

Mind your head!

luggage tag

DEPARTURES

	TIME	GATE
PARIS	3:30	2
WORK VILLE	4:00	1
VENICE	4:02	3
NEW YORK	5:15	1
LONDON	5:30	3
TOKYO	6:00	2

lots of luggage

porter

"These are the check-in counters. Passengers show their tickets here, and also have their baggage weighed and tagged with its destination," Rudolf explains. "Each passenger receives a boarding pass to enter the plane at the gate."

check-in hostess

ticket

boarding pass

"The airport terminal is like a small Busytown," says Rudolf. "There are shops that sell books, toys, and flowers. And there's a police station, a post office, and a first-aid center, too!"

"Is there a bathroom, Mr. Von Flugel?" Sally asks.

BANANAS

CHAPEL

WATCHES

TOYS

FLOWERS

While they wait for Sally, Lowly asks if there is also a restaurant at the airport. "Travel always makes me thirsty!" he laughs.

As soon as Sally returns, Rudolf drives up the escalator to the restaurant.

RESTAURANT

restaurant

catering truck

boarding gate

WORKVILLE

passenger bus

kerosene fuel is pumped into tanks in the wings

baggage train

fire extinguisher

ho

cleaning truck

paper to recycle

bottles to recycle

126

"Wow! What a view!" exclaims Huckle.

electric generator

passenger bus

plane positioner

catering trucks delivering meals

pier

waiting room

tail

door

fuselage

cleaners cleaning the inside of the plane

pilot and copilot

wing

baggage compartment

jet engine

baggage loader

baggage handler

flight crew arriving

ramp agent

tractor

Rudolf drives over to the control tower.
Please take care driving up the stairs, Rudolf.

catering kitchen
preparing meals

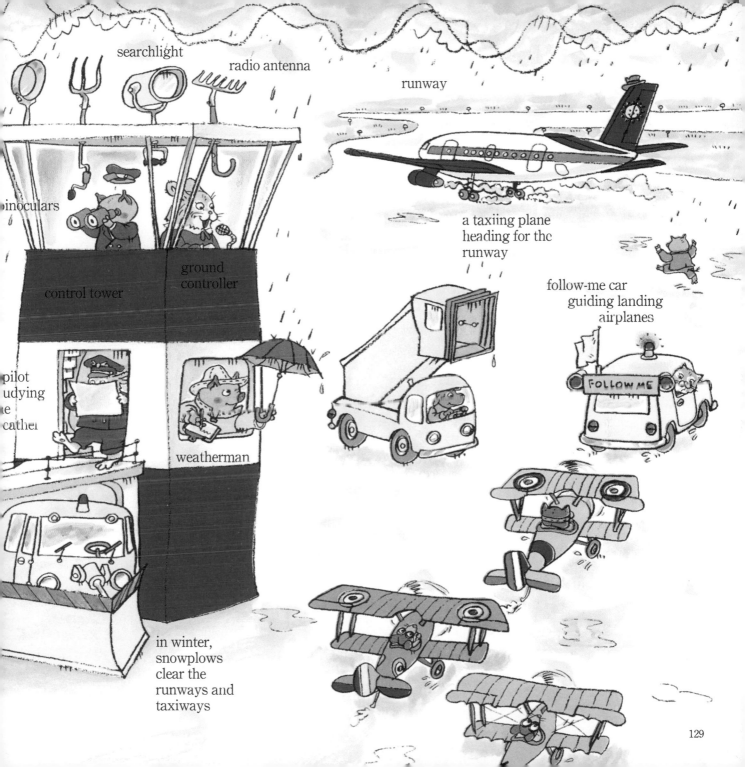

searchlight

radio antenna

runway

binoculars

control tower

ground controller

a taxiing plane heading for the runway

follow-me car guiding landing airplanes

FOLLOW ME

pilot studying the weather

weatherman

in winter, snowplows clear the runways and taxiways

129

"From up here, each plane receives instructions by radio—where to park and when to take off and land," Rudolf explains. "At night and in fog, you can still see every plane on this radar screen."

radar antenna

DON'T STEP ON THE GRASS.

radar screen

"Busy Air Flight One, you're clear for takeoff," says the ground controller into the microphone.

The big plane races down the runway and soars into the sky. *Whooosh!*

Hey! No running on the runway!

wind sock showing the wind's direction

ground controller

"Mr. Von Flugel," says Sally, "you know so much. Can you tell me what that funny-looking thing over there is?"

cargo plane

"Ach! I almost forgot!" cries Rudolf. He drives across the runway, past a cargo plane being loaded with freight containers.

132

airplane hangars

luggage trolleys

"These are the hangars, Sally," says Rudolf. "Inside, airplanes are parked and repaired."

"Thank you, Mr. Von Flugel," Sally replies. "But what's *that*!?" she asks, pointing.

freight containers

"Ach! *This* is my Bratwurst Balloon!" Rudolf says. "Quick! Hop in before you get wet!"

"Wow!"

MUSTARD

"Look out, everyone!" calls the ground controller. "Here comes the Bratwurst Balloon!"

Soon they are high in the sky.

"Look! There's our house!" says Huckle. "Mom! Dad! Look up!" he calls.

No, look *out,* Rudolf! Your Bratwurst Balloon is about to burst.

Bump! They all land safely on Huckle's front lawn.

"Well, Rudolf, that was a perfect landing," says Father Cat.

"Thank you, Mr. Von Flugel!" say Huckle, Sally, and Lowly.

"This has been the best afternoon ever!"

Richard Scarry's
NICKY GOES TO THE DOCTOR

Nicky Bunny was going to the doctor.
He waved to all his friends as he and
his mother drove through town.

"I'm going to see the doctor,"
he shouted.

AUTO TRANSPORTER

POLICE

Nurse Nightingale met them at the door. "It's so nice to see you," she said. "Won't you please come in?"

While Nicky was waiting for the doctor, Nurse Nightingale showed him a book. It told him the right things to eat to help him grow big and strong.

143

Then it was time to see Dr. Doctor.
"Hello, Doctor," said Nicky.
"Hello, young fellow," said Dr. Doctor.
"Please take off your shirt and slacks so I
can examine you."

145

"My, how you've grown
since you were here last,"
said the doctor. "Even
your ears."

"You've gained weight, too," said Dr. Doctor.
"That's because I always eat everything
Mommy gives me," said Nicky.

Nicky had to laugh when the doctor examined his stomach. "Excuse me, Doctor," said Nicky, "I'm ticklish."

"Perfectly normal," said Dr. Doctor.

"Now say 'A-a-ah,'" said the doctor.
"A-a-ah!" said Nicky, and the doctor looked
down his throat.

The doctor looked at Nicky's ears. He took a
long look, because Nicky had long ears.

The doctor put his stethoscope on Nicky's back, to
listen to him breathing. Whish-whoosh, whish-whoosh,
the air went in and out of Nicky's lungs.

Then the doctor put his stethoscope on Nicky's chest.
Thump-thump, thump-thump went Nicky's heart.

"Listen to my heart," said Dr. Doctor.
And Nicky heard the doctor's heart go
thump-thump, thump-thump.

The doctor tapped Nicky's knee with a little
hammer, and Nicky's foot jumped up by itself.
"That's a very fine knee you have, Nicky,"
said Dr. Doctor.

Then Dr. Doctor gave Nicky a shot.

"Ouch!" said Nicky. "I don't like shots."

"Nobody likes shots," said the doctor, "but we need them sometimes to help us stay healthy and well."

"I know," said Nicky.

"Now we'll test your eyes,"
said the doctor. He showed Nicky
some pictures.

"I see a carrot, a pear, a
strawberry, a banana, and a
blueberry," said Nicky. "I like
the carrot the best."

"You have good, sharp eyes,"
said Dr. Doctor.

"Well, Nicky," said Dr. Doctor, "you're healthy and growing nicely. Get dressed and Nurse Nightingale will give you a balloon."

"Thank you, Doctor," said Nicky.

At home, Mrs. Bunny told Mr. Bunny how much Nicky had grown. "Just keep it up," said Mr. Bunny proudly to Nicky. "Some day you'll be as tall as I am!"

161

Then Nicky told his brothers and sisters all about
his visit to the doctor. And they all wanted to go, too.

"Be patient," said Mrs. Bunny. "I can't take you all
at once. You'll have to take turns."

The children were patient. They all finally did visit
the doctor, and he found them all healthy and well.

Wasn't that nice?

Richard Scarry's Busy Activities

Make your own Lowly Worm! You will need paper, scissors, and crayons.

How to make Lowly:

1. Place your piece of paper on top of this picture of Lowly.

2. Trace Lowly. Don't forget his bow tie!

3. Use your crayons to color Lowly's face, hat, clothes, and shoe.

4. Use your scissors to carefully cut along the outline of Lowly.

Now you have your own Lowly Worm to play with!

START HERE

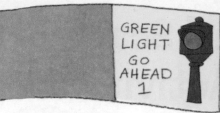

GREEN LIGHT GO AHEAD 1

HURRY, FIREFIGHTERS! PUT OUT THAT FIRE!

STEP ON GAS GO AHEAD 1

50
75

ROAD REPAIR GO BACK 2

BLOW SIREN GO AHEAD 2

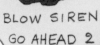

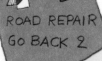

HEN IN ROAD GO BACK 1

You will need a penny, a nickel, and a quarter. How to play:

1. Let your friend choose the penny or nickel as his or her game piece. The other one is yours. Place your coins on the firehouse.

2. Flip the quarter to see who goes first.

3. Take turns flipping the quarter again. If you flip heads, move forward one space. If you flip tails, move forward two spaces.

4. If you land on a space with writing on it, follow the instructions.

5. The first firefighter to reach the fire wins!

FLAT TIRE
GO BACK 2

STOP FOR GAS
LOSE 1 TURN

FIRE CHIEF SAYS "GO FASTER"
GO AHEAD 3

KID OFF ROAD
GO BACK 3

FINISH

LOSE YOUR HELMET
GO BACK 1

CROSSWALK
LOSE 1 TURN

SERGEANT MURPHY STOPS TRAFFIC
GO AHEAD 2

Lowly loves ice cream. Do you?

Make your own ice cream!
You will need (have a grown-up help you):

1/2 cup of milk

1 tablespoon of sugar

1/4 tablespoon of vanilla extract

crushed ice

6 tablespoons of rock salt (not table salt; rock salt can be found at the grocery store)

a pint-size ziplock bag

a gallon-size ziplock bag

What to do:

1. Mix the milk, sugar, and vanilla extract in a bowl.

2. Put the mixture into the smaller ziplock bag and zip it closed.

3. Fill half of the bigger ziplock bag with ice.

4. Add the rock salt.

5. Put the small bag into the large bag. Zip the large bag closed.

6. Shake it up! Keep shaking! Shake the bag for ten minutes. Make sure the bags don't break open.

7. After ten minutes, remove the smaller bag from the larger bag. Pour the ice cream into a bowl.

8. Enjoy your delicious ice cream!

A Visit with Tillie

Make your own telephone to call Tillie and friends!

You will need:

2 plastic cups
a sharpened pencil
3–10 yards of string
2 paper clips

What to do:

1. Have a grown-up help you poke a hole in the bottom of each cup with the pencil.

2. Pull the end of the string through the hole of one cup from the outside.

3. Tie the end of the string to a paper clip.

4. Pull the other end of the string through the hole of the other cup from the outside.

5. Tie the other end of the string to the other paper clip.

6. Hold on to one cup. Have a friend hold the other cup.

7. Walk away from each other until the string is tight.

8. Have your friend speak into her cup while you put yours to your ear. Can you hear what your friend says?

Tillie called some friends and invited them to her house.
Make Tillie's house so you can visit her!
You will need:
an empty cardboard milk or juice carton
glue
scissors
newspapers
paint
a paintbrush

What to do:

1. Rinse the empty carton out with water and let it dry.

2. If the top of the carton is open, glue it closed.

3. Have a grown-up help you cut off the bottom of the carton.
   Make sure it can still stand evenly on the table.

4. On one side of the carton, cut up from the bottom and then cut over to make a
   door. Make a crease so that the door opens and closes easily.

5. Place the carton on top of the newspapers so that you don't get paint on the table.

6. Use your paints and paintbrush to paint Tillie's house! What color do you want the roof
   to be? What color do you want the door to be? Don't forget to paint windows so that Tillie
   can see the lovely view.

Something's different! Point to the character who is different in each row.

Time to set sail!

Do you see any of the items listed below? When you find each one, point to it.

an anchor
3 teapots
2 forks
a tricycle
4 flags
a bucket
3 chef's hats
a flight of stairs
flowers
an hourglass
a clock

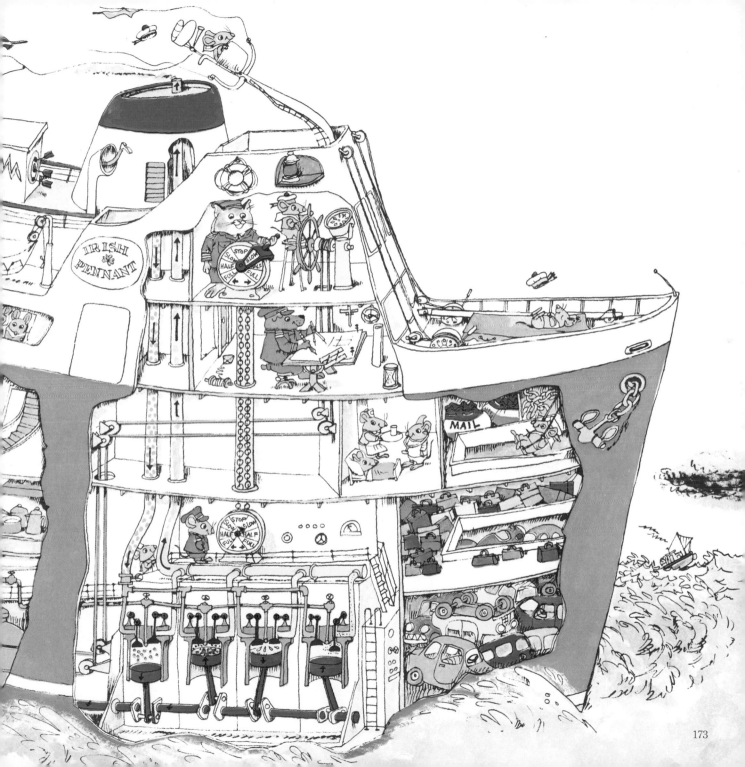

Make your own finger puppets!

You will need paper, scissors, tape, and crayons. What to do:

1. Cut a strip of paper long enough to wrap around your finger.

3. Wrap the strip around your finger and tape it closed. Set it aside.

3. Put another piece of paper over the puppet you want to make. Trace the outline.

4. Use your crayons to draw a face and clothes on your puppet.

5. Carefully cut your puppet out with the scissors.

6. Tape your puppet onto the loop of paper you set aside earlier so that the hole is at the bottom.

Now you have your own finger puppet!